LEGENDS

of

OZ

Dorothy's Return

LEGENDS OF OZ

Dorothy's Return

Cover by
Eric Shanower

Cover Colors by
Joana Lafuente

Collection Edits by
Justin Eisinger
& Alonzo Simon

Collection Design by
Tom B. Long

3 1969 02245 7278

Special thanks to Travis Rutherford, Kirsti Tichenor, and Summertime Entertainment.

ISBN: 978-1-61377-905-7

www.LEGENDSOFOZMOVIE.com

17 16 15 14   1 2 3 4

Ted Adams, CEO & Publisher
Greg Goldstein, President & COO
Robbie Robbins, EVP/Sr. Graphic Artist
Chris Ryall, Chief Creative Officer/Editor-in-Chief
Matthew Ruzicka, CPA, Chief Financial Officer
Alan Payne, VP of Sales
Dirk Wood, VP of Marketing
Lorelei Bunjes, VP of Digital Services
Jeff Webber, VP of Digital Publishing & Business Development

www.IDWPUBLISHING.com
IDW founded by Ted Adams, Alex Garner, Kris Oprisko, and Robbie Robbins

Facebook: **facebook.com/idwpublishing**
Twitter: **@idwpublishing**
YouTube: **youtube.com/idwpublishing**
Instagram: **instagram.com/idwpublishing**
deviantART: **idwpublishing.deviantart.com**
Pinterest: **pinterest.com/idwpublishing/idw-staff-faves**

The Jester and the Magic Scepter

~ Written by ~
Denton J. Tipton

~ Art by ~
Blair Shedd

~ Colors by ~
Joana Lafuente

~ Letters by ~
**Neil Uyetake,
Shawn Lee,
& Chris Mowry**

~ Series Edits by ~
Denton J. Tipton

Chapter 1

IN WINKIE COUNTRY. THE WICKED WITCH OF THE WEST'S CASTLE.

KNOCK KNOCK

KNOCK KNOCK KNOCK

...IT'S TIME FOR AN EXTREME MAKEOVER.

YOU'LL FIND THAT *MY* TASTES ARE MORE... SOPHISTICATED.

BUT SOME THINGS I'LL *DEFINITELY* BE KEEPING.

ALSO UNLIKE MY SISTER, I WON'T MELT AT THE SIGHT OF...

NOW LISTEN UP, MONKEYS! OTHER THAN LETTING HER BE MELTED, YOU SERVED MY SISTER WELL.

AND YOU'RE GOING TO DO THE SAME FOR ME—

—UM, OTHER THAN LETTING ME BE MELTED.

ARE YOU LISTENING TO ME, YOU?!

"THE WICKED WITCH'S BROOMSTICK HAS BEEN STOLEN?"

...NO PRINTS FOUND

NOT PICKING UP ANY FINGERPRINTS ON THE GLASS CASE.

...NO PRINTS FOUND

NOTHING BACK HERE.

I'M PICKING UP A SCENT... IT'S...

...FLYING MONKEYS!

NOW I'M REALLY SCARED!

I'M NOT SCARED OF A LITTLE MONKEY WITH WINGS!

WHY WOULD THEY DO THIS?

I ASSUMED THE FLYING MONKEYS WOULD KEEP TO THEMSELVES AFTER BEING FREED OF THE WITCH'S CONTROL. THEY MUST HAVE A NEW MASTER.

BUT WHO?

I SUSPECT WE'LL FIND OUT SOON ENOUGH.

YES! THE BROOMSTICK!

OR WHAT'S LEFT OF IT.

WELL, LET'S SEE WHAT I CAN DO ABOUT THAT...

...WITH MY PUDDLY SISTER'S SPELL BOOK!

AND WITH THIS ORB, MY WICKED SISTER'S POWER WILL BECOME MINE!

FROM A MAGICAL BROOMSTICK THAT FLIES...

...THE FORM OF A JESTER'S SCEPTER ARISE!

YEOW! HOT! HOT! HOT!

Chapter 2

THE EMERALD CITY.

WE COULD HEAR *CHANTING*, AND SOME SAID THEY SAW A *VISION* OF A JESTER IN THE CLOUDS.

JESTER, HUH? DIDN'T THE WICKED WITCH HAVE A BROTHER WHO WAS A JESTER?

I THINK YOU'RE RIGHT, TIN MAN.

BUT CONTINUE WITH YOUR REPORT, MUNCHKIN.

THE STORM WAS TERRIBLE. THE RAINWATER WASHED AWAY OUR FIELDS AND BRIDGES.

"WORST OF ALL, A FARMER REPORTED SEEING *FLYING MONKEYS* CARRYING OFF THE MAYOR OF MUNCHKIN LAND. WE ARE WITHOUT A LEADER IN THESE TROUBLING TIMES."

HAVE COURAGE, MY MUNCHKIN FRIEND. WE'LL FIND THE MAYOR AND TAKE CARE OF THIS JESTER.

WON'T WE, SCARECROW?

OF COURSE, LION!

NOW RETURN HOME TO HELP WITH REPAIRS AND LEAVE EVERYTHING ELSE TO US.

LEAVE EVERYTHING UP TO US? OH, THAT'S TOO MUCH PRESSURE! MY HEART WOULD *NEVER* TAKE THE STRESS!

CALM YOURSELF, TIN MAN. WE'RE GOING TO GET HELP. WE'RE GOING TO *NEED* IT.

BECAUSE IT SEEMS THE JESTER HAS STOLEN HIS SISTER'S BROOMSTICK AND HARNESSED ITS POWER.

AND THE ONLY ONE WHO CAN STOP THE JESTER IS...

...DOROTHY GALE OF KANSAS!

DAINTY CHINA COUNTRY.

BUT IT IS CUSTOMARY, PRINCESS.

THE GRAND PALACE.

AND I'M SURE YOUR SUBJECTS WOULD FEEL *LESS FRAGILE* IF YOU HAD A PRINCE BY YOUR SIDE.

WHAT?! DO YOU THINK I'M *INCAPABLE* OF PROTECTING MY SUBJECTS?

NOT AT ALL, YOUR ROYAL HIGHNESS. YOU HAVE MANY *SUITORS* WHO ARE... SUITABLE.

YOU MEAN THAT DEPLORABLE *WINKIE?* IF HE WERE MORE FULL OF HIMSELF, HE'D BURST.

WELL, THERE'S ALSO THAT NICE *MUNCHKIN*.

WHY, HE'S SO JUMPY IT WOULD BE LIKE A LITERAL TEMPEST IN THE TEAPOT. HE'D NEVER DO.

WELL, PRINCESS, THERE ARE OTHER...

...WHAT'S THAT NOISE?

SOLID GROUND? SHIFT AND SHAKE...

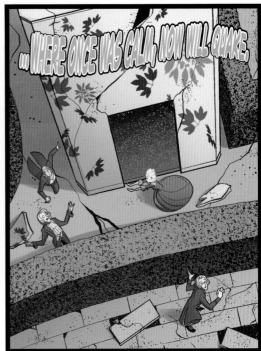

...WHERE ONCE WAS CALM, NOW WILL QUAKE.

HAHAHAHAHAHA!

ALL OF OZ WILL FEEL THE JESTER'S WRATH!

SINCE THE WIZARD LEFT ME IN CHARGE OF OZ, I HAVE ACCESS TO HIS LABORATORY AND ALL THE WONDROUS WORKS WITHIN.

OH, I *DO* MISS THE GREAT AND POWERFUL OZ.

NOW, DON'T CRY, TIN MAN. YOU'RE *RUSTING!*

SORRY, SCARECROW. GO AHEAD WITH YOUR PRESENTATION.

THANK YOU, TIN MAN.

WELL, I'VE USED THE WIZARD'S GADGETS AND GEAR TO CONSTRUCT A MACHINE THAT WILL BRING DOROTHY BACK HERE TO OZ.

I CALL IT...

...THE RAINBOW MOVER!

VERY IMPRESSIVE, SCARECROW. HOW DOES IT WORK?

WELL, THAT'S THE PROBLEM. IT *DOESN'T* WORK.

NOT *YET*.

IT NEEDS A RAINBOW.

WHERE ARE WE GOING TO FIND ONE OF THOSE?

I THINK WE NEED TO SEEK THE ADVICE OF GLINDA, THE GOOD WITCH.

NOT EVEN A HAIRLINE CRACK. WE WERE VERY LUCKY.

WELL, THE REST OF THE COUNTRY WASN'T SO LUCKY, PRINCESS.

OH, YES. OF COURSE. WAS ANYONE BROKEN?

NO, PRINCESS. THERE WERE A FEW WHO WERE CRACKED, BUT NONE ARE BEYOND REPAIR.

SECURE THE BORDER AND LET NO ONE IN OR OUT UNTIL WE LEARN WHAT CAUSED THE QUAKE.

YES, YOUR HIGHNESS. AND WE MUST PREPARE IN CASE IT HAPPENS AGAIN.

HAPPENS AGAIN?

PERHAPS I SHOULD CONSIDER FINDING A SUITOR...

ONCE WE REACH GLINDA'S CASTLE, SHE'LL KNOW WHERE TO FIND A RAINBOW...

...BUT FIRST WE HAVE TO CROSS THE MUNCHKIN RIVER.

I CAN'T GET WET! I'D BE SO RUSTY; ALL THE OIL CANS IN OZ WOULDN'T SAVE ME!

WELL, WE DON'T HAVE A BOAT...

...PERHAPS WE CAN SWING ACROSS?

WELL, WE FOUND A TREE TALL ENOUGH, BUT WE STILL NEED ROPE.

WOULD A NICE, STRONG VINE WORK?

I THINK IT WOULD. WAIT. WHO SAID THAT?

YOU ARE AT THE GATES OF DAINTY CHINA COUNTRY. STATE YOUR NAME AND BUSINESS!

I THOUGHT YOU'D BE BIGGER.

I'M SCARECROW. AND THIS IS TIN MAN AND LION. WE WANT TO FOLLOW THE YELLOW BRICK ROAD THROUGH YOUR NATION.

WE ARE IN A STATE OF EMERGENCY. NO ONE GETS IN OR OUT. ORDERS OF THE CHINA PRINCESS HERSELF.

YOU'LL HAVE TO GO AROUND.

BUT THAT COULD TAKE WEEKS. WE NEED TO TALK TO GLINDA, THE GOOD WITCH OF THE SOUTH, AND FIND OUT WHERE WE CAN GET A RAINBOW.

I'VE HEARD THE CANDY MAN IN CANDY COUNTY CAN MAKE RAINBOWS. YOU CAN FIND HIM IN THE VALLEY OF BONBONS.

I'M THE OFFICIAL GAMEKEEPER. IT IS MY JOB TO SEE THAT YOU OBEY THE RULES AND FINISH THE GAME ON TIME.

MY NAME IS LION. HAVE YOU SEEN MY FRIENDS THE TIN MAN AND SCARECROW?

THEY'RE PLAYING THE GAME! LET ME SEE... ...MY, HOW TIME FLIES! THEY BEGAN THE GAME FOUR HOURS AGO. THAT JUST GIVES THEM TWO HOURS LEFT TO FINISH THE GAME, OR THEY LOSE.

WHAT HAPPENS IF THEY LOSE?

THE SAME THING THAT WILL HAPPEN TO YOU, AS YOU'RE ABOUT TO PLAY THE GAME OF THE MAZE, TOO. YOU HAVE SIX HOURS, JUST AS THE TIN MAN AND SCARECROW HAVE, OR YOU ALL WILL VANISH FOREVER.

AND WHAT IF I DON'T WANT TO PLAY YOUR GAME?

THEN YOU AUTOMATICALLY LOSE BY FORFEIT.

STRAW. SCARECROW MUST BE THIS WAY.

IT'S A GOOD THING YOU FOUND US WHEN YOU DID. I JUST RAN OUT OF STRAW.

SINCE WE WERE HEADED EAST WHEN WE WERE CAUGHT IN THIS MAZE, THE EXIT SHOULD BE IN THAT DIRECTION. WE MUST FOLLOW ANY PATH THAT TRAVELS EAST—

—THE DIRECTION OF THE RISING SUN.

THERE! IT'S THE EXIT!

PERMIT ME TO INTRODUCE MYSELF. I'M THE SCHOOLMASTER. THANK YOU FOR WINNING BACK OUR TOWN OF PURPLEFIELD.

THE WICKED WITCH OF THE WEST LEFT A SPELL ON OUR TOWN LONG AGO. NOW, THANKS TO EACH OF YOU, THE SPELL IS BROKEN AND WE'RE FREE AGAIN.

PLEASE STAY AND CELEBRATE WITH US TONIGHT!

NO, THANK YOU. WE MUST BE GOING—

—EAST! I SEE THE MERINGUE MOUNTAINS TO THE EAST!

Chapter 3

AT LAST... *CANDY COUNTY.*

IT'S JUST BEAUTIFUL...

WHY ARE YOU GETTING ALL CHOKED UP, TIN MAN? YOU DON'T EVEN EAT CANDY, OR ANYTHING ELSE, FOR THAT MATTER.

COME ON, GUYS. I THINK THIS IS THE *VALLEY OF BONBONS,* WHERE WE'LL FIND THE *CANDY MAN.*

I SURE COULD GO FOR SOME BREAKFAST FIRST...

EATING CANDY HERE IS A DIRECT VIOLATION OF SECTION EIGHT, PARAGRAPH TWELVE OF PENAL CODE ONE SIX ONE SIX FIVE.

PLEASE STEP AWAY FROM THE CUPCAKE, SIR.

AND WHO ARE YOU?

MARSHAL MALLOW. SECOND IN COMMAND OF THE GARRISON AT CANDY COUNTY.

WHAT'S YOUR BUSINESS HERE IN CANDY COUNTY?

WE'RE HERE TO SEE THE CANDY MAN.

WELL, I'D SAY YOU'VE SUCCEEDED!

WE HAVE?!

INDEED! YOU'VE ALREADY SEEN SEVERAL CANDY MEN. EVERYONE IN CANDY COUNTY IS MADE OF CANDY!

OH. *THAT* CANDY MAN.

ACTUALLY, WE'RE LOOKING FOR ONE CANDY MAN IN PARTICULAR, *THE* CANDY MAN. WE WERE TOLD HE LIVES IN THE VALLEY OF BONBONS.

YOU KNOW HIM, THEN? CAN YOU TAKE US TO HIM?

IT'S MY DUTY TO SERVE AND PROTECT.

I'VE ALREADY PROTECTED, SO NOW I'LL SERVE... AND ESCORT YOU TO THE VALLEY OF BONBONS.

JUST DON'T EAT *ANYTHING.*

AS YOU CAN SEE, THERE IS THOROUGH SIGNAGE.

FORWARD... MARCH!

FUDGE. POPS. LEMON DROPS.

FUDGE. POPS. LEMON DROPS.

I COULD REALLY DO WITHOUT THE CANDY CADENCE CALL.

FUDGE. POPS. LEMON DROPS.

FUDGE. POPS. LEMON DROPS.

BOY, IS THAT CHANT ANNOYING!

I'D RATHER LISTEN TO YOU MONKEYS FIGHTING OVER A BANANA PEEL!

NOW WHAT ARE THAT SCARECROW, THAT LION, AND THAT TIN CAN UP TO? ARE THEY TRYING TO FIND *DOROTHY GALE*, THE WITCH SLAYER FROM KANSAS?

SHE'S THE *ONLY* PERSON WHO COULD THREATEN MY PLAN!

I THOUGHT I TOLD YOU TO GET RID OF THIS!

WELL, I WAS PLANNING TO SEND A MESSAGE TO CANDY COUNTY ANYWAY.

NOW I CAN KILL TWO BIRDS WITH ONE STONE, AND SCARE DOROTHY GALE'S FRIENDS FROM THEIR MEDDLING.

BLAZING SUN, RAGE AND ROAR...

...RISING HEAT, MAKE TEMPERATURES SOAR!

ALL THIS MARCHING IS STARTING TO MAKE ME SWEAT!

UH... THANK YOU.

THINK NOTHING OF IT.

IT'S BACK TO NORMAL. YOU DON'T SUPPOSE THE JESTER IS RESPONSIBLE?

I *DO* SUPPOSE.

THE JESTER?

HE'S THE BROTHER OF THE WICKED WITCH OF THE WEST. HE HAS HER MAGIC BROOMSTICK, AND PLANS TO USE IT TO RULE OVER OZ.

I MUST REPORT THIS TO GENERAL CANDY APPLE AT ONCE!

CONTINUE ON THIS HEADING AND YOU'LL SOON REACH THE VALLEY OF BONBONS.

SURELY WE'RE CLOSE NOW.

XX MAGNIFICATION

WAIT, THERE'S SOMEONE.

ING FOR RAINBOWS

HELLO, THERE! WE ARE LOOKING FOR THE CANDY MAN.

HOW DO YOU DO? *I'M* THE CANDY MAN. I MAKE SOME OF THE MOST DELICIOUS DELECTABLES IN ALL OF CANDY COUNTY.

PLEASED TO MEET YOU! I'M SCARECROW. THIS IS LION AND TIN MAN. WE'VE COME ALL THE WAY FROM THE EMERALD CITY SEEKING YOUR HELP TO SAVE THE LAND OF OZ.

WHY, I DON'T KNOW HOW I'D BE ABLE TO HELP WITH THAT AT ALL. BUT...

...WAIT. ARE YOU EATING CANDY?!

WHERE DID YOU GET THAT? IT'S CLEARLY POSTED THAT TAKING CANDY IS EXPRESSLY FORBIDDEN!

UNLESS, OF COURSE, IT IS GIVEN TO YOU BY THE CANDY MAN HIMSELF. THEN YOU MAY INDULGE TO YOUR HEART'S CONTENT!

SORRY, WE DIDN'T SEE ANY SIGNS ABOUT CHEWING GUM.

HMM. THAT *IS* A STICKY WICKET.

WE'RE ON A VERY IMPORTANT MISSION TO SAVE OZ FROM THE PERSON WHO CAUSED THE HEATWAVE. HE'S TRYING TO TAKE CONTROL OF OZ.

IT'S TRUE. WE NEED A RAINBOW AND WERE TOLD THAT YOU HAVE THE CAPABILITY TO MAKE THEM.

YES, THE BEST IN ALL OF OZ! JUST FINISHED A BATCH THIS MORNING.

SWEET!

WELL, IT LOOKS LIKE THE APPLE OF MY EYE FELL FOR MY FALSE SUMMONS TO THE EMERALD CITY.

APPLE OF YOUR EYE? NONSENSE, YOU CUR! YOU CARE NOTHING FOR ME, AND EVEN LESS FOR MY MEN. YOU'RE ROTTEN TO THE CORE!

BUNCH OF SAVAGES IN THIS CASTLE!

WELL, NOTHING SOOTHES THE SAVAGE BEAST LIKE A LITTLE MUSIC. CARE TO DANCE?

HA HA HA HA HA!

OF COURSE! YOU JUST NEED—

—WHITE LIGHT AND A PRISM.

PRISON? SOUNDS SCARY!

NO, A PRIS-*EM*. IT'S A—

—TRIANGULAR PIECE OF GLASS. WHEN WHITE LIGHT ENTERS THE PRISM, IT COMES OUT THE OTHER SIDE SEPARATED INTO THE COLORS OF THE RAINBOW: RED, ORANGE, YELLOW, GREEN, BLUE, INDIGO, VIOLET.

AND I THOUGHT SCARECROW TALKED A LOT.

BY THE WAY, MY NAME IS WISER.

GO FIGURE.

WELL, THANK YOU FOR YOUR HELP, WISER. I'M SCARECROW, AND THIS IS LION AND THE TIN MAN.

BUT WE MUST BE GOING. IT'S A LONG TRIP BACK TO THE EMERALD CITY AND WE'RE IN QUITE A HURRY.

FAREWELL, SCARECROW, LION, AND TIN MAN!

GOODBYE!

SO WHERE ARE WE GOING TO FIND ONE OF THESE PRISMS?

I RECALL SEEING ONE IN THE WIZARD'S CHAMBER. IT WILL WORK IN THE RAINBOW MOVER PERFECTLY.

I FINALLY SEE CLEAR SKIES AHEAD.

Chapter 4

LITTLE HELP, GUYS?!

THEY WON'T KEEP HIM UP LONG IF I HAVE ANYTHING TO DO WITH IT!

GOT YOU!

BUT WHO'S GOT *YOU*?!

GERONIMO!

HEY!
I NEED
THAT!

OH, I'M
SORRY. I'M
SO SORRY.

COME ON, TIN
MAN. WE HAVE TO
MAKE A BREAK
FOR IT!

scOS
•BRAIN POWER: 100%
•STRAW LEVEL: MIN - REROUTING
•FIRE DANGER: MED

SUITABLE GAP NOT FOUND!

AND I'M NOT SEEING AN OPENING AT ALL.

THEN WE MAKE OUR FINAL STAND HERE.

DID YOU HAVE TO SAY FINAL?

WAIT! I'VE GOT THIS!

OF COURSE! THE FIGHTING TREES!

THEY MUST REMEMBER THE LAST TIME WE CAME THIS WAY AND YOU GAVE THEM A THRASHING WITH YOUR AXE, TIN MAN!

LET'S BOLT!

THE CASTLE OF GLINDA, THE GOOD WITCH OF THE SOUTH.

OH, GOOD. SCARECROW, LION, AND TIN MAN MANAGED TO FLEE INTO THE FOREST. WE STILL HAVE HOPE.

ONLY DOROTHY CAN SAVE OZ FROM THE EVIL JESTER.

WHILE THE JESTER HOLDS THE SCEPTER, EVEN I'M POWERLESS TO STOP HIM.

WHA—?

THE EMERALD CITY.

I KNOW I SAW THAT PRISM AROUND HERE SOMEWHERE...

EUREKA!

HEY, GUYS! I FOUND IT!

"...AND TRANSPORT HER HERE FROM KANSAS."

HONK HONK HONK

WILL THESE HICKS JUST GET OUT OF MY WAY ALREADY?!

SINCE WE'RE RUNNING THESE PEOPLE OUT OF THEIR HOMES, THE LEAST THEY CAN DO IS *RUN.*

YOU REALLY SHOULD BUY YOURSELF A SENSE OF HUMOR.

NOW, LET'S SEE THE NEXT HOUSE TO CONDEMN...

...AH, THE GALE FARM...

CONDEMN

ISSUED BY: 712th

CASE NUMBER: LL 90-0.

In the Matter the property des

Gale Farm, 567 East Cedar

TO TERED ERTY

Henry Gale

Affidavits by C e Cour

unsafe and/o e due to t

"...IT SHOULD BE JUST UP THE ROAD HERE."

WELL, GOOD MORNING, SLEEPYHEAD.

≥YAWN≤ MORNING.

DOROTHY GALE, UNCLE HENRY AND I WERE SO WORRIED ABOUT YOU. WHEN YOU DIDN'T MAKE IT INTO THE CELLAR, WE THOUGHT WE'D LOST YOU.

AT FIRST, I THOUGHT THE HOUSE WOULD BE RIPPED TO PIECES. THEN I CALMED MYSELF, AND DESPITE THE ROARING WINDS, I FELL FAST ASLEEP. AND THE HOUSE LOOKS TO HAVE MADE IT OUT FINE, TOO.

WELL, LET'S HOPE SO.

WHAT DO YOU MEAN?

IT WAS A POWERFUL TORNADO, DOROTHY. THERE'S BEEN A LOT OF DAMAGE.

DOROTHY! WAIT!

DOROTHY!

❧ Art Gallery ❧

Art by
Eric Shanower
Colors by
Joana Lafuente

Art by
Eric Shanower
Colors by
Joana Lafuente

Art by
Eric Shanower
Colors by
Joana Lafuente

Art by
Eric Shanower
Colors by
Joana Lafuente

Art by
Blair Shedd

Art by
Blair Shedd